THE TOWER THAT FELL

by Rosemary Luling Haughton

with illustrations by the author

Paulist Press
New York/Mahwah, N.J.

Book design by Céline M. Allen

Cover design by Jim Brisson

Library of Congress Cataloging-in-Publication Data

Haughton, Rosemary
    The tower that fell / by Rosemary Luling Haughton : with
illustrations by the author.
        p.   cm.
    ISBN 0-8091-3686-4 (alk. paper)
    1. Babel, Tower of--Fiction. 2. Bible. O.T. Genesis XI, 1-9-
-History of Biblical events--Fiction. I. Title.
PR6058.A84T69   1997
823'.914--dc21   96-46097
                                                            CIP

Published by Paulist Press
997 Macarthur Boulevard
Mahwah, New Jersey 07430

Printed and bound in the
United States of America

Chapter 1

Very, very long ago, in a very far away land, there lived a little girl whose name was Star. She lived in a City called Babel. Star's father was a builder and built houses, and her mother wove beautiful cloth of many colors. They lived in a little house with a garden of flowers and vegetables around it. She had a friend, a little boy called Wind who lived just across the street, and her mother had woven some red cloth for a shirt for him. Wind's father and mother were bakers; wonderful smells of fresh bread wafted across the street early every morning, and Wind used to bring Star the first loaf out of the ovens. Wind also had a grandmother who was a healer. She used to collect herbs and make medicines to cure sick people.

Star liked to watch her mother weaving, and she was even beginning to learn to spin the thread her mother wove, but she also liked to follow her father and watch him and the other builders building houses. It was exciting to see them laying the bricks so neatly and the walls rising higher and higher.

Every day Star's friend Wind used to bring a basket of fresh rolls from his parents' bakery to the builders for their lunch, wherever they were working, and Star often helped him to carry them. Then both children would sit on stacks of bricks with the masons and listen

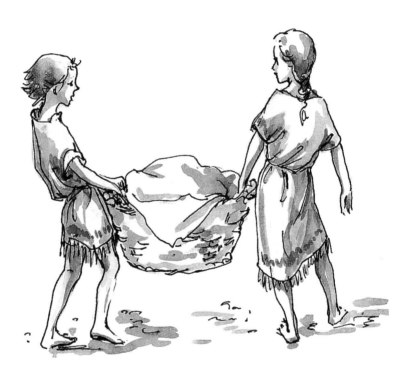

to them talking. They talked about the greatness of the City, and how clever they thought the people were. The children's parents also said things like that to each other and to the children. So the children thought that their City was perfect, nothing could be better.

One day, Star and Wind had to carry the rolls farther than usual because the builders were beginning work on a new building on the other side of the City. After that, every day they had to walk a little farther because the walls the men were building stretched so far—far longer than the walls of a house, or even a palace! They were as long as a street! So by the time the children got to the place where the men were working they were tired, and glad to sit down and watch the work for a while. When the men stopped work to eat their lunch Star asked her father, "What are you building? It's so long!"

"That's only the beginning!" he told her. "This building will be very long and very wide, but much, much higher than that! As high as heaven!"

"Why?" piped up Wind, round-eyed.

At that all the men stopped work for a moment and looked at each other and at the children, but nobody answered. At last a man who had rolled-up papers in his hands and looked important said, "The Wise

Ones have commanded it. These are plans for the biggest Tower that was ever built!" He patted the rolls of paper and smiled. But Star asked, "Why?" again. The man didn't answer but frowned.

"You shouldn't ask questions," he said, and turned away and shouted at the men, and they all began working very hard.

So Star and Wind went home. They both went to Wind's parents and asked, "Do you know why the builders are building a house as high as the sky?" Both parents looked worried, but Wind's mother said in a whisper, "Maybe it's so that we can talk to God."

"Does God want to talk to us?" asked Star, but Wind's father frowned and told her not to ask questions.

So the children went to Star's mother. "Why are the builders building the Tower up to heaven?" they asked. Star's mother also looked worried. "I know the Wise Ones told them to build," she said. "They say God is up there, and we need to talk to God. The Wise Ones tell us all we need to know — they know best," she added quickly, and would say no more.

Next day, after they had delivered the rolls and seen how high the Tower was getting, Star and Wind went to the Big House where they knew the Wise Ones lived, and knocked on the door. They had never been there before but they knew that the Wise Ones lived there, and that the Wise Ones told everyone what to do and how to live. Sometimes they had seen one or two of the Wise Ones, dressed in white robes and with long beards, walking through the streets, and everyone bowed as they passed because they knew that it was the Wise Ones who told the people how to make the City so great and beautiful. However, Star and Wind were not afraid of the Wise Ones because they had always been told, "They are good, they care for us."

A very old man they knew was a Wise One because of his white beard and long white robes opened the door and looked down at them in surprise, but he was quite kind. "What do you seek?" he asked.

Star said, "We have come to ask why the masons are building the Tower up to heaven. Nobody explains."

At that, the old man frowned. "You are very young," he said, "so you may be forgiven. Nobody explains to you because your questions are not real questions. There is nothing to ask questions about because everything is as it should be. Those who try to find answers where there are no answers are unwise." He frowned and added, "They could even be called wicked, but you are too young for that, and I will tell you about the Tower to prevent harm to the City from your foolish questions. Come in."

The Wise One took them into a great marble hall with strange signs carved in the walls. Other Wise Ones were walking to and fro, carrying what Star and Wind knew were books, because they had been told about them, but they had never seen them before and did not know what they were for. The old man sat on a big chair and gave the children cushions to sit on, and he gave a wise smile instead of the frown, but that made the children feel worse than the frown had done.

"Listen carefully," he began, "because I am Wise and we who are Wise have all knowledge and know what is best. The great Tower is being built up to heaven because, so far, God has stayed in heaven. Heaven is so high that we suppose God has not known how great and perfect our City is, and how Wise are we who guide it. Heaven is very high up, so we are building a Tower high enough so that we can climb up to meet God and share our wisdom with Him. Then God will truly know how Wise we are and God will be one of us and there will be no questions."

"What questions?" asked Wind, puzzled. "You just said there *were* no questions!"

The Wise One frowned again and his face turned red.

"You didn't hear right," he said. "You are only children and don't understand. Of course there are no questions because we are so wise that everything is known and everybody understands everything."

"We didn't," said Star and Wind together, but the Wise One looked so angry that the children scrambled up and out of the door and ran home as fast as they could. After that they refused to carry the bread to the builders, and Wind's parents grumbled and had to find someone else to carry it.

When Star's father came home every evening he talked a lot about how high the Tower was getting, and how it would soon reach heaven, and indeed Star and Wind could see it in the distance as it rose over the roofs of the other buildings, higher every day, with steps going up the outside so people could climb up. But as the days went by Star's father talked less and less, and looked worried and unhappy. When his wife asked him what was the matter he glared and told her to mind her own business.

Chapter 2

As the days passed Star and Wind grew more and more miserable, because in both families there were quarrels, or long silences. They noticed that other grownups in their street and in the market no longer chatted and laughed together but ignored each other. The children asked their parents what was wrong, but they just looked more worried and angry. "Nothing's wrong," they said, or "How could anything be wrong?" and "Only bad children ask questions!" So Star and Wind were afraid and stopped asking.

Then one day a messenger came to their street. He was dressed in white robes, and came from the house of the Wise Ones. Everyone gathered round while he read from a long roll of paper.

"In ten days the Tower to reach heaven will be finished," he proclaimed, very loudly. "Everyone is invited to a great celebration. By then the Tower will touch heaven and the Wise Ones will mount the Tower and respectfully ask God to be our chief speaker at the banquet. Then we will lay the final bricks, and the day will be a holiday, and all should come to the bottom of the Tower in their best clothes."

There was great excitement, and most of the grownups began to look quite cheerful.

"Now we know for sure everything is perfect. The Wise Ones know all!" they said. "God will be one of us! God will be pleased! We need not have worried!"

"Will God tell us new things?" asked Star, but her father was not pleased.

"Of course not," he said, "there are no new things to tell. The Wise Ones already understand everything and they teach us what we need to know. And now that we've almost finished the high Tower God will understand that the Wise Ones truly know." But he still didn't sound very happy, and Star's mother cried and pretended she hadn't.

Ten days later everyone put on their very best clothes and went to the Tower. All the Wise Ones were there, all with long white beards and special gold edges to their white robes. Trumpets sounded and the procession of Wise Ones began to mount the steps of the Tower, which was so high that clouds hid the top.

13

Higher and higher the Wise Ones went. As the people watched them they began to look quite small, and still they went up.

"When will God talk?" Wind asked his father, but his father only told Wind to keep quiet. Time went on. Star and Wind were bored and began playing noughts and crosses in the dirt to pass the time. Other people, too, were sitting down and beginning to eat their holiday picnics, but they didn't talk much.

Suddenly, a very bright light flashed across the sky and everyone sprang to their

14

feet.

There
was a huge
roaring sound
like thunder and
lions mixed and the
earth under their feet
trembled. Then a brick fell
out of the cloud that hid the top
of the Tower, and then another, and
when the people squinted up they saw
that the Wise Ones at the lower end of the procession
were scrambling down the steps at a great rate. More
bricks fell, and although nobody was hurt the crowd
was scattering quickly away from the Tower and people
were crying out in fear. The stones fell faster and the
people could see more and more of the Wise Ones
scrambling down and could hear them crying out even
above the noise of the falling bricks. Some of the Wise
Ones even jumped from high up and fell to the ground
and Star saw them being picked up by their friends,
crying and moaning, with cut heads, or carried off on
ladders left behind by the builders. Soon there was no
one left near the Tower as the ground shook and the
stones fell faster and faster. Nobody knew what had

happened to the Wise Ones who had been in the front of the procession and got highest up into the clouds.

Star and Wind and their families ran with the rest, back to their own street. People were pale with fear and some were crying.

Star was frightened herself but also puzzled, and she went over to Wind's house to talk to him about what had happened. He was sitting alone on a bench outside his house, and she gave him a hug.

"Do you think God wasn't pleased about the Tower?" she asked. But instead of answering Wind looked at her with his mouth open.

"What's the matter?" she said impatiently. "We aren't hurt but all the grownups are upset and I don't know what's going on."

But Wind only began to giggle, and then he said something—but he seemed afraid, and she couldn't understand him.

"Listen to me!" she shouted, and stamped her foot, but Wind began to cry, and turned and ran into the house. She followed him and said to his mother, "Wind won't talk to me. What is he afraid of?"

Wind's mother turned to Star and shouted at her in an angry voice, but Star couldn't understand. Wind was making noises to his mother, and she turned to Star and

shouted at her, but her shouts made no sense either. Star tried to make her listen, but she only took a broom and chased Star out of the house.

Star ran out crying, and saw two of the Wise Ones hurrying down the street. "Perhaps they've come to explain what happened," she thought, "and they'll make Wind better."

"Please help! I don't understand!" she cried to them. But they turned angry faces to her and when they opened their mouths and shouted she heard only senseless, angry noises, and soon they disappeared down the street. Sobbing, she took refuge in her own house.

There, her mother was sitting on a stool, crying, and her father was waving his arms, but Star sobbed out, "I don't understand, Wind is talking nonsense and so are other people and even the Wise Ones."

Her mother put her arms round her and said, "Oh, my poor child, something terrible is happening!" But her father only made strange noises and cried, too, and rushed out.

When Star and her mother crept out to see what was going on they saw people coming out of all the houses and everyone was shouting and waving fists or weeping, and nothing they said sounded like real words to Star. She could see Wind and she called to him, but he only looked at her in a scared way and then turned his face away.

However, after a few moments Star and her mother were relieved to hear some voices in the crown shouting real words! Quickly they pushed their way toward those voices, crying "Can you understand us?" Soon a little group had separated from the crowd, and though things still seemed terrible and frightening it was wonderful to be with people who understood what you said.

"It's all because of the Tower!" someone said.

"Maybe God didn't like it!" said someone else.

"Look!" cried another, pointing, and they looked and saw that where the Tower had loomed over the City only a cloud of dust was slowly rising.

"God is angry with us," someone said.

"Nearly everyone has gone mad, they can't speak real words!"

"Perhaps God has made them mad as a punishment!"

"Perhaps God is angry because the Tower went up to the place where He lives!"

"But *we* aren't crazy," said one man, "so God isn't so angry with *us*!"

"But we won't be safe here with all those bad, crazy people!" said another. "We'd better leave here before they attack us and we'd better be careful not to do anything God won't like or He might punish us worse!"

The little group of people looked at the other people crowded in the street and saw that it wasn't a crowd anymore, it had split up into several groups like their own, and the people in the groups seemed to be talking to each other, and each group was looking at all the others with fear, and some were shaking their fists. Star saw some of the men go into their houses and come back with spades and clubs and axes. Other people were running to their homes and women were gathering up cooking pots and hurriedly pulling washing off the lines. In one place two groups actually began to fight, whacking each other with sticks and even slashing with knives, and soon there were people on the ground with blood on them.

Then Star's mother said to the group that could understand her, "Let's not wait to be attacked, let's take what we can and go." The rest nodded and they all hurried to collect whatever they could pile on donkeys and hand-carts or carry in bundles. They rounded up a few goats and pigs too, but only a few because other people had taken most of them. As they worked, out of the corners of their eyes they could see other people doing the same thing all down the street, and there were fights going on about animals and even children. They could hear shouts and banging from other parts of the City, so they knew this was happening everywhere.

Star's mother packed up her loom and baskets of bright colored wool, and Star cried as she worked, because of fear and of losing her father and also from sadness about her friend Wind. But she and her mother were very busy and soon they were on their way, leaving the house and the street and City that had been everything they knew, that they had always believed was perfect and could not change. At first, as they hurried away, they had to pass through the same streets as other groups of people, and there was a lot of shouting and some people were hurt, but as soon as they came to the edge of the City the groups took different directions, to get away from each other.

Star looked back and saw that the streets were now empty and quiet as far as she could see. Only the dust cloud over the collapsed Tower was rising up and beginning to blow away into the sky. As they went on their way Star looked back and picked out the group where Wind was, and she could recognize him by his red tunic. She watched them getting farther and farther away, and smaller and smaller in the distance. Finally, when she could only just distinguish Wind's little figure in his red tunic she jumped up on a cart and waved and waved. And, after a moment, she saw Wind's hand waving back. Then he was gone, out of sight.

Chapter 3

Many years passed. Star and her mother and the other people in their group found a distant valley where they could settle, and grow crops and build homes. Star grew up and married and had children, and her children grew up too and had families of their own. By that time there was a real town in that place. The people, who all understood each other, called themselves "The Blessed Ones" because they believed they were the only ones not punished by God. And because God had punished all the Others so severely they knew that God was very powerful, and severe, so they must be very careful never to do anything God didn't like. Then the only problem was that they were never quite sure what God didn't like, and so they were afraid of God. They wished they had the Wise Ones to tell them what God wanted, but the Wise Ones had never been seen after the day when the Tower fell.

So all the people were very careful to do everything the way they had done it before and never to do anything different, for they believed that since God had not punished them as much as the Others it must be because they had done things in ways God liked. And they were careful not to do any of the things they remembered being done by the Others, such as making healing medicines, or building with brick—all their homes were of clay and straw instead.

Star had become a weaver like her mother, and indeed she became so good at it that she taught many others, and the people of that land had the most beautiful bright colored clothes with tassels and patterns on them. When Star was old and her grandchildren came to see her she showed them pictures she made with her weaving, and told them stories. She showed them the woven pictures of the Tower that was built, and of the stones falling off it and in one corner a picture of a little boy in a red tunic. She told them the story and at the end of the story she always said, "And so my friend Wind waved to me, and I never saw him again. Perhaps he has grandchildren like you, but they are among those God punished, so they are not good, and that makes me sad."

There was another thing that made her sad, though she didn't speak of it, nor did the other older people. This was that, in their land, many babies died of strange fevers and nobody could cure them. Some of the older people remembered being told by their parents that in the City they had left, there had been people who cured fevers. But no one dared to try to do this because this was something the Others had done, the ones whom God had punished. They believed that to heal fever would make God angry. If people died it must be God's will, they told each other, but many of them were sad, and wondered secretly.

One of Star's grandchildren was a little girl who was called Little Star, after her grandmother. She loved her grandmother's stories, and thought about them a lot. Little Star and her family lived in a village some way from the town, and Little Star used to help care for the goats, so sometimes she had to walk quite a long distance to find good pasture for them. When she climbed the hills and looked far across the country she wondered whether, somewhere over there, there was another child who was Wind's grandchild, and she longed to meet that child, though she was a little afraid, because she had been taught that all the Other people from the City were punished by God, and were bad and crazy and couldn't talk Real Talk.

It was true, of course, that in all those years when Star's people had been making themselves a home, the other people from the City had also found places to settle. What Little Star did not know was that all of those Other people also believed that they were the only ones whom God had spared when He punished the City. They too believed that God was terrible and severe. Each group believed themselves to be specially spared the madness and evil of the rest, and so they called themselves names like "The Chosen," or "People who Talk Sense," or "Healthy People." In time these groups grew, and began to enlarge their fields and build new villages and explore farther and farther.

So it happened that, while Little Star was climbing the hills with her goats and gazing across the hills and trying to imagine another child who might be Wind's grandchild, that other child was not far away. He was Wind's grandson, and his name was Breeze, and he belonged to the ones who called themselves "The Healthy People." They knew that they were specially chosen, and not like the other mad, bad people, because among them were some whose great-grandparents, like Wind's grandmother, had brought from the City a skill in healing. They knew how to use herbs to cure illness, and they taught it to others. Breeze was one of those who was apprenticed to an old woman who was a healer, so he wandered the hills, not to herd goats, but to collect the herbs to make medicines.

But nobody in that land knew how to weave, so they made clothes out of animal skins, or felted wool, and though they kept the old woven garments that had come from the City they only used them for special occasions to remember the great City from which they had come. They said that not weaving any new clothes was what God wanted, for they knew Others had been able to weave and they had been punished, so not being able to weave must be God's will, and they must not question that. But the clothes brought from the City were not cursed because they had been made before the punishment. However, Breeze's grandfather, Wind, had kept an old red shirt which was too ragged for special occasions, so he let the boy wear it when he was off by himself. Breeze knew the story of how Wind had left the City and waved to his friend Star, so he had a special love for the old shirt.

One day, in his search for healing herbs, Breeze wandered farther than usual, and saw a slope ahead that he had not climbed before. He thought he would get a good view from the top, so he climbed up. The weather was warm and the slope was steep, so when he got to the top he sat on a rock to get his breath, and looked across the hills all around. Suddenly he noticed some goats on the side of the valley below him, and a little girl with them. He knew she was not from his people because her clothes were different. Perhaps, he thought, she is one of the crazy people that God punished. She was walking among the goats, and he could hear that she was singing to them, though he couldn't understand the words. Then he saw her sit down on a rock and unfold a cloth with her food in it. She didn't seem particularly crazy. After a while, he waved.

As Little Star sat on her rock and took a bite of bread and goat's cheese she looked around, thinking that she should soon turn back toward home. Then she saw a little boy sitting on a rock on the hill opposite, and he was waving. And he was wearing a red shirt— rather faded and ragged but still red. She remembered the little figure in the corner of her grandmother's tapestry pictures, and her heart beat fast. Suddenly she waved back.

Then, almost without thinking, both children got up, and Breeze clambered down the slope and Little Star ran across the valley, with the goats inquisitively following. At the bottom of the slope the children stopped and looked at one another silently. Little Star smiled, and Breeze smiled back. Little Star tried to remember the things about the punished people, but this boy looked much like any of the boys she knew, except that his shirt was so ragged. "Hallo!" she said, forgetting

that such a boy
would not be able
to understand Real
Talk.

Breeze grinned,
because what she said
didn't make sense—
after all, the Other Peo-
ple couldn't be expect-
ed to talk Real Talk—but he knew what she meant.
"Hallo," he said back, and it sounded peculiar to her but
it was clear what *he* meant. "I'm Little Star," she said, and
then realized he would not know what that meant, so she
bent down and scratched a picture of a star in a bare patch of
earth, and pointed to the sky and then to herself. Breeze
looked, and nodded, but he couldn't draw a breeze, so he
waved his hand through the air and blew with his
mouth, and pointed to himself and they both laughed,
because it was so funny.

By that time they had both forgotten about being
afraid, but they were full of curiosity and questions that
couldn't be answered. It was very frustrating. They did
manage to indicate more or less where each one lived,
and even to draw in the dust what kind of houses they

lived in. But evening was coming and both knew they had to go home, so they agreed to meet again, by pointing to the ground where they stood and waving their arms to indicate coming back.

That evening, Little Star went to her grandmother and told her what had happened. She felt Star was more likely to listen and not get upset at the idea of meeting one of the Others. She told her about the old red shirt, and that the boy's name was something like "Windy" or "Breeze," and that he wasn't at all wicked or crazy and that she wanted to meet him again and try to understand more. Little Star waited, and her grandmother gazed ahead as if she were looking far away.

"Perhaps you're right," she said at last. "And perhaps we have been wrong. Wind was my friend; why should he and the other people with him be bad? Don't tell anyone else yet, but go and learn all you can."

That is what Little Star did, and she and Breeze found ways to understand one another. They taught each other words for "water" and "rock" and "sun" and "bread" and "goats" and a lot more—and soon they could speak to each other, not very well but enough to manage. And so both of them realized that the speech of their own people was not the only Real Talk, and that perhaps the Others were not crazy after all.

As the days passed the two children talked of many things, and one of the things they talked about was clothes, for Breeze admired Little Star's beautiful woven dress very much, but he was afraid of it too. "My people don't make that." He pointed to her dress, but didn't touch it. "My father says God doesn't want us to make clothes like that. We use animal skins but we keep the Holy Clothes from the City for special days. Only grandfather's shirt was too old for that so he lets me wear it, if no one sees. I like it."

Little Star was surprised. "My people all have clothes like this, to wear every day. I am learning to weave them. It is God's will."

"Is that a different God?" Breeze wondered.

One day they talked about their families. "I have a little sister," said Breeze. "She is just beginning to walk." Little Star looked sad. "I had an older brother and a younger brother but the older one died."

"How did he die?" asked Breeze.

"He became very tired, and he was wet and hot and then dry and he cried and said nonsense things, and he couldn't eat, and then he died," Little Star said sadly. "It was God's will."

"My teacher would have given him medicine and he would have got better!" said Breeze. "Why didn't your healers give him medicine?"

"We haven't any healers," Little Star said, staring. "They say people die because it's God's will. If we make medicines God might punish us like..." Then she stopped because she realized she had nearly said, "...like you."

"That must be a different God," Breeze cried. "I think the God of your people must be a bad God. He wants people to die when it's quite easy to heal them!"

"And I think your God must be crazy if He won't let you wear nice woven clothes!" shouted Little Star and for a minute the children glared at one another, afraid and confused. But somehow their friendship had become too important for them to let it be spoiled. Both of them were having a lot of new thoughts, that were hard to deal with.

When Little Star went home that night she want to her grandmother's house, and told her all that had happened. "I don't think he is bad or mad," she said finally, "he's just like me in most ways. But now I can't believe all the things people say about the Others! They can't all be bad if they can cure babies so they don't die! Can our God be good if He doesn't let us cure the sick people? Grandmother, I'm so confused!"

Star sat for a long time, pondering. "Oh, Little Star," she said, "you and your new friend are not the only ones who ask these questions, but most dare not ask them out loud. In the City, before we could not understand one another, we believed that there were no questions because we thought we knew all that could be known and had nothing to learn, not even from God. So when the Tower was destroyed and we could not understand one another we who fled believed that only the Others were wrong, and the punishment was all their fault, so we must be careful never to ask questions or change anything we remembered. But—I think we don't remember very well. Now, you and your friend are asking the questions. Perhaps something new is beginning. But you must be very careful—some people may be angry if they know that you are friends with one of the Others, and try to hurt you—and him."

Little Star told Breeze what Star had said, and they were both careful not to say anything at home about what was in their minds, though that was very difficult. And they went on meeting and talking together when they could, and asking strange questions.

Then one day Little Star's baby brother became sick. He cried and wouldn't eat and his skin was very hot.

Little Star's mother cried and tried to comfort him, but the neighbors just said, "It is God's will. He will die."

Little Star didn't waste any time or wait for the goats. She sped over the hills as fast as she could go, to look for Breeze, and finally found him so near his own village that she could see the smoke from its chimneys.

"You mustn't come so close!" he said to her. "If they saw you in those clothes they would know you were one of the Others, and maybe hurt you!"

"Never mind that," Little Star cried, all out of breath. "You must come! My baby brother is sick—just like the older one was. They say he will die! Please bring medicine for him! Quickly!"

"But—I'm not a healer, I haven't learned yet," Breeze said, but Little Star interrupted him.

"You can ask your teacher, can't you? If you can't heal him, maybe she can!"

Poor Breeze stared at her and said nothing for a moment. Then he said, "Wait there!" and ran back toward the village.

For Breeze, like Little Star, had found he needed to share his secret with someone, and that someone was his teacher, a healer called Smoke, and she had listened and comforted. So now, Smoke understood at once that this was a very important moment, and she

took a bottle with some medicine made of herbs and put it in her leather pouch and followed Breeze. Of course she could not understand Little Star's words but all three understood what they were doing and that it was dangerous.

By the time they reached the village it was already dark and most people were indoors, so Little Star was able to lead them to her home without anyone seeing. Inside, Little Star's mother, who was called Moonbeam, was rocking the baby who cried fretfully, and her father stood by the fire with his head turned away. Little Star touched her mother's shoulder.

"I've brought someone who can make our baby well," she whispered, "but keep quiet so the neighbors don't hear." Both parents looked around, and Moonbeam stared at the brown-skinned, gray-haired woman who had entered her home. "Who is she?" she asked. "Can she really help?"

But Little Star's father, called Bush, stared angrily. "What curse have you brought, child?" he said—but he spoke low. "This isn't one of our people—she's one of the Others! The baby will die because God wills it—to let the Others interfere would be wrong and God would punish us!" But he looked at the baby, who gave a feeble wail, and he shut his eyes.

Moonbeam was looking at Smoke. "Can you heal Him?" she said, and Smoke understood her meaning and nodded; she came forward and took the baby gently and looked him over, and then turned to Breeze, who was behind her. "Tell the mother I will give the little one some medicine and he will sweat and he will get better," she said, and Breeze translated in his odd way of talking their language, and both parents stared at him and at Smoke while she gave the baby the medicine, but they did not try to stop her.

"Tell her she should bathe the child with warm water and give him water to drink and wrap him warmly, then he will sleep. And give him more of the medicine in the morning," Smoke said to Breeze, and he translated. Moonbeam nodded and took the bottle, but Bush said quickly to Little Star, "They must leave! If people saw them here they would blame me." So Little Star guided Smoke and Breeze quickly through the darkness to the edge of the village.

Next day, Little Star took the goats out as usual, and when she met Breeze she gave him a bag, and in it were two beautiful woven robes, one for Smoke and one for Breeze.

"The baby is better," she said. "In the night he sweated, and after that he was cool and he slept. My mother and father are very glad, and they want you to have the clothes—but they are afraid, too, that God will be angry with them. But I don't believe God is angry—I think we didn't understand God. My grandmother Star thinks so too."

"It's time we found a way to talk to each other—and talk to God," said Breeze, "but it's going to be difficult."

Chapter 4

From that day, things began to change among the peoples of Little Star and Breeze. As Breeze had said, it was very difficult because so many were afraid. They were afraid of God and afraid of the Others and afraid of change, because they never knew if something different would make God angry, and they would be punished. Very bad things would happen.

One bad thing happened when Smoke put on the beautiful woven dress that the healed baby's parents had sent. Although she knew it might cause trouble, she wore the dress because she wanted people to understand what she had done. "They are not evil," she said. "We can learn from each other—we can give them knowledge of healing and they can teach us to weave clothes and make things with leather." But some of the neighbors were afraid, and they set fire to Smoke's

house and beat her and drove her out. So she went across the hills and went secretly to Star's house and Star took her in, and with the help of Little Star the two women began to speak to each other.

Not long after, when some neighbors saw that Little Star's baby brother had not died they were afraid, and some of them beat Bush and threatened to kill the baby. But somehow nothing else happened, because some families began secretly to wonder whether if their children became sick they might want them not to die. Some even began to wonder if God really wanted babies to die, but they didn't say so aloud.

Meanwhile, Little Star began to tell other children about what she had discovered, and some listened and asked new questions, and some were timid and afraid. The children told their parents and some were thoughtful and felt happy about the new ideas, and some were afraid and angry, and soon there were fights and people were hurt. Star began talking to older men and women, a little at a time, and introduced some to Smoke, and there was more argument but, since there were so many on both sides of the argument, after a while people stopped fighting because they realized they might destroy all the people. As for

Little Star and her friends, they talked and thought, and consulted Star and Smoke and talked more. Whatever some grownups did, they were beginning to know some new things and think and act in new ways.

The same kind of thing was happening among Breeze's people. At first he hid his beautiful woven tunic because he was afraid of being beaten like Smoke, but he showed it to his grandfather, Wind, and to a few of his own friends, and they saw how beautiful it was. "I don't see why it's wicked to make things like that," one said. Breeze showed it to his parents, and after a while they began to feel he might be asking some good questions. They spoke to their friends about it, and some listened. But it was the children who were bold and shared new thoughts.

"Wouldn't it be good if we could learn to do this?" said one. "They can do things we can't, and Breeze says *they* don't know how to heal people, so we could teach them."

"But they are different from us—they are the Others," said another. The children looked at one another in fear because they had always been taught that to be different was wrong.

At last Breeze said, "What if being different is *good*—what if the grownups didn't understand God properly—what if we really *need* different people?"

That was a strange and dangerous new idea, but after a while more people were asking these questions, and of course others were angry about the questions, but that didn't stop them.

Little Star and Breeze still used to meet in the hills and tell one another what was going on. One day, after they had talked for some time, they had an idea.

"Let's get the other children to meet each other," Breeze said, "so they can see the Others are just like themselves."

"But they are also *different*," said Little Star, "and —and now perhaps they'll be able to see that that's *good!*"

So it was arranged, and groups of children from both peoples began to meet—at first a very few brave ones, and then more and more. They looked at each other and touched one another, and began to learn each other's languages. They came secretly because they were afraid some parents wouldn't have let their children go, and would have punished them when they found out, but in fact most of the parents knew where

they had gone, but pretended they didn't; some really wanted them to go, though they didn't dare to say so.

When they could speak to each other easily enough the children asked one another questions about their customs and how they lived, and each group heard that the others had been taught to hate and despise all Others, and to believe that God had chosen only themselves, while Others were punished.

"But they must have got the story wrong!" said a very little boy one day. That was a scary idea, but the other children listened, and after a while some nodded. It made sense.

"They told us God didn't like people wanting to talk to Him," said an older boy. "They said God was afraid that if they built the Tower right up to heaven, people would be as great as God, and that is why He knocked the Tower down."

Some began to wonder about the Tower.

"You know they said people in Babel thought they knew everything—and people who think they know everything make mistakes and blame other people," said one older girl, and the others nodded wisely.

"Maybe it wasn't God who knocked the Tower down, maybe it just fell because it wasn't well built, and there was a big storm," another suggested.

"And they told us God made the Others crazy to punish them—but maybe the grownups were all upset and blamed each other."

It was rather confusing, but one thing was clear: the old story didn't make sense of what they knew of each other.

"Perhaps we can tell a better story," said Little Star, who had been talking to Star and hearing her memories of the City. "We can begin to make a new story and when we know more we can make it even better."

They all thought this was a good idea, and so every time they met they told a bit more of the story, making suggestions and asking questions. In between they talked to older people like Wind, to see what they remembered, but it was the children's own story, which they needed in order to understand how to live together. For they knew, now, that they couldn't go on being separated. They were different, and they needed all the differences.

When the children told the new story, they found that they were talking about a different kind of God, a God who didn't punish but loved the people.

"Perhaps people will understand God better if we tell them God is kind like a good mother," said one little boy.

"But lots of fathers are good too," said a little girl; "if we call God 'She' instead of 'He' perhaps some of the fathers will think God doesn't like them."

"Well, remember we said the story will *change*," said an older girl. "Just for a while, let's tell about a mother kind of God, so people will understand about God caring.

When everyone really knows that we can change if we want to, it won't matter whether we use 'He' or 'She.'"

So that was what they agreed to do.

In all the weeks and months that the children were making this new story, life was also gradually changing between the two peoples, because news of how Moonbeam's

baby had recovered spread, and though some said it was against God's will others remembered people they loved who had died, and perhaps needn't have died. Smoke ventured to go back home, and though some glared at her, nobody hurt her, and some even helped her rebuild her house. Many admired her beautiful woven robe and a few even visited Little Star's village and asked to learn weaving. And Smoke herself went back and forth, and taught healing to a few people in Little Star's village, and nobody tried to kill her, though some shut their doors when she went past and said what she

did was evil. Each group learned different ways to build, too.

After a long time, the children's new story was finished enough for them to dare to share it with any grownup who would listen. They knew, though, that in time it would need to change as they, and their own children, asked new questions and learned to understand better. So the story was told in all the villages and

towns, and some said it was nonsense and bad, but others felt it was much more likely to be true than the old stories. From that time on, both peoples began to know one another and learn from one another, though many were still afraid God wouldn't be pleased. They discovered, in time, that there were still many more Others, who had Different languages and Different skills, and that it was possible to know them and learn from them. Still, sometimes, people were afraid, and even fought and killed each other, but more and more among all of them began to learn the new story, and take comfort from it and even add to it. They knew that being Different was good.

As for Little Star and Breeze, when they grew up they were married, which caused a lot of upset for a while, but they didn't care. And they taught their children the new story.

Chapter 5

The New Story

This is the new story that the children told:

Once upon a time there was a great City called Babel, and it was full of people who made beautiful and useful things and had great knowledge. And God blessed them and God loved the good things they learned and made.

And the people thanked God for their City and their skills and their knowledge and were eager to learn of the God who was so far beyond their learning and yet always with them and caring for them.

But some of the people became so proud of all they knew and all they could do that they began to think there was nothing more to learn, and that they could do anything they wanted. They would not ask questions because that would mean they didn't know everything, and they stopped thanking God and delighting in the gifts God gave them. Instead, they thought they had a right to all the good things because they were so clever and good, and that God was obliged to do things the way they wanted.

They decided to build a Tower up to heaven so that they could meet God and make sure God knew how great they were and would do things the way they wanted. They had forgotten that God was with them and among them as well as in heaven.

In those days when God walked through the City She was very sad. She tried to talk to the people and make them happy and full of delight in all that they could learn and do, together with Her. But they didn't see Her because their eyes were dazzled with the beauty they had made, and they didn't hear Her because their ears were stuffed up with the noise of their own cleverness, so they kept on building the Tower to show how they knew everything and had all power. God said, "I can't let these poor people spoil all that we have made together. There must be a way to show them that there is always more to learn, and that we can only do that together."

God waited a long time hoping the people would change. But in the end the Tower got so high it was top-heavy, and the foundations were not strong enough because the builders did not ask the right questions about building. So, when there was a shaking of the earth, which sometimes happened around there, the Tower fell down. God was sad for the people, but She hoped they would understand Her and themselves better. But God saw that the people were still so afraid to share with Her and with each other that they couldn't understand and were even more afraid. They were so afraid that they couldn't even talk to each other and work it out. So they all ran away in different directions with a few others whom they could understand, but what they could understand, of course, was not much.

And each group that ran away believed that God had done all this to punish them because She was jealous of their power and didn't want them to be near Her. Each believed all the others were the cause of the trouble and were bad and punished by not being able to talk sense.

But when God made it so that people were divided by their speech She also made it so that each group had some special gifts and skills that others didn't have. And that wasn't a punishment but an opportunity.

God was very sad that the people were still telling such untrue stories about God and about each other, and She wept over them, but She was patient because She knew that it takes a long time to change the minds of people who are both frightened and conceited.

And so it came to pass in time that children from each of the separated peoples began to meet, and to learn to speak to one another, and through them knowledge and skills were exchanged, and evil thoughts began to change.

God was glad that Her plan had worked. Her people were beginning to know some important things:

- that difference is good,
- that there are good and bad people everywhere,
- that there is no end to the beautiful things we can learn and make, if we do it together,
- that God does not punish us, but loves us,
- that we don't need to build a Tower to meet God because God is always with us and hears us and teaches us, if we listen.

God knew it would take a long time for everyone to understand these things, and She was often sad because so many did not understand and still feared Others and still told bad stories about God. But She was happy because of the ones who did understand, and she spoke to them and spent time with them. And God said, "One day everyone will understand and I shall live freely among my people forever."